The Twelve Dancing Princesses

For Seren Shelley — Mary Hoffman
For my parents — Miss Clara

Barefoot Books
2067 Massachusetts Ave
Cambridge, MA 02140

Adapted from the fairy tale by the Brothers Grimm
Text copyright © 2012 by Mary Hoffman
Illustrations copyright © 2011 by Miss Clara, first published in France
Le Bal des douze princesses © Hachette Livre / Gautier-Languereau, 2011
The moral rights of Mary Hoffman and Miss Clara have been asserted

First published in the United States of America
by Barefoot Books, Inc in 2012

Graphic design by Louise Millar, London
Color separation by B&P International, Hong Kong
Printed in China on 100% acid-free paper
This book was typeset in Carlton and Janson
The illustrations were prepared as scale models,
which were photographed and digitally enhanced

ISBN: 978-1-84686-838-2

Library of Congress Cataloging-in-Publication Data:
available under LCCN 2012009598

1 3 5 7 9 8 6 4 2

The Twelve Dancing Princesses

Retold by Mary Hoffman

Illustrated by Miss Clara

Barefoot Books
step inside a story

Contents

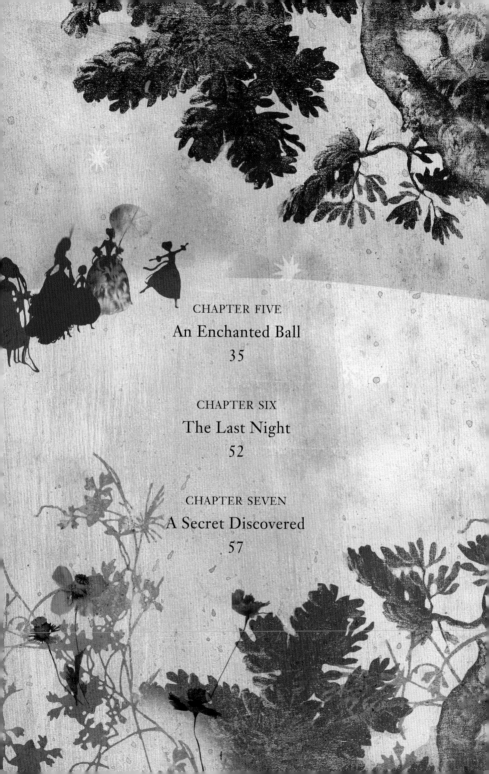

The Twelfth Princess

Once upon a time, there was a king who was lucky enough to have eleven beautiful daughters, each one as lovely and as lively as the last. The king and the queen loved their family and rejoiced in their good fortune. To each daughter, they gave the name of a flower — there was Violette, Delphine, Iris, Jessamine, Lilou, Véronique and Verveine, Eglantine, Amarante, Marguerite and Rose. Every year the queen bore another child, and every year the royal trumpeters climbed the winding staircase to the highest turret in the palace and blew their trumpets to let the people know that they had another princess to welcome and adore.

But in the twelfth year, the queen fell ill as she gave birth to her last daughter. The people of the kingdom heard the trumpets announce the royal birth, but fast upon their call there came a dark slow drumbeat from the palace drummers. Then the king sent his messengers through the land to tell his people that their queen had died in childbirth.

The king named his youngest daughter "Amandine" because the almond tree, from which he chose her name, can give bitter fruit as well as sweet.

The queen's final words to her grieving husband were, "Take care of our girls, my dearest. They will need a lot of looking after as they get older." And then she closed her eyes for the last time.

How right she was! By the time the eldest, the lovely Princess Violette, was eighteen, the palace was swarming with suitors. They were all the younger sons of other kings, hoping to gain a crown as well as wife.

Chapter Two

A Mystery

The king was very fond of his daughters, and he wanted them all to find good husbands. But he had a terrible problem, and try as he might, he could not solve it.

The king had given his princesses a large and lofty chamber in one of the wings of the palace. Every night they went to bed in the vast room they shared, and the king would come and tuck them in, reading a story to the littlest one, Princess Amandine. He would kiss each one of them in turn, say good night and leave them to get ready to go to sleep. He would close the door quietly behind him and turn the key in the lock to make sure the princesses stayed there till morning.

But every morning the princesses' beautiful silk and satin slippers had been reduced to rags and tatters. Obviously, they had been out dancing — but where? And how? And who with? The palace

was kept firmly bolted and guarded at night and any stray princes were swiftly sent out into the courtyard as soon as darkness fell.

The three palace shoemakers were kept busy every day making fresh slippers for the twelve princesses. Every evening, new slippers were placed in their bedchamber, but every morning, the maids who came to wake the princesses found the slippers worn down to rags.

Every mouse in the palace knew she could find nice soft scraps of material to line her nest if she visited the princesses' bedroom in the morning. There were silks and satins of every hue, pattern and texture, buckles and pearls, and ribbons and tassels that had come loose.

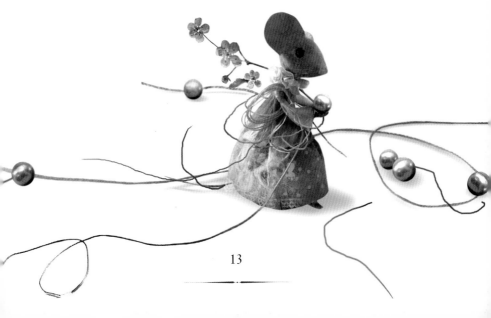

And as for those hardworking shoemakers, when they came into work, they sighed over the ruined slippers and, with heavy hearts, started to make new ones all over again.

The king was frantic. His daughters were pale and yawning, just as if they had danced the night away, and their ruined slippers told the same story. But when he asked them what had happened, they merely shook their sleepy heads as if under some enchantment.

Well, if this was magic, the king decided he would beat it with cunning. He issued a proclamation that if anyone could solve the riddle of the princesses' nighttime adventures, that man could not only choose which princess he would like to marry, but also look forward to inheriting the king's throne.

"I might as well make all those young princes do something useful," the king thought. Then he added to the proclamation that anyone who attempted this task and failed should lose his life.

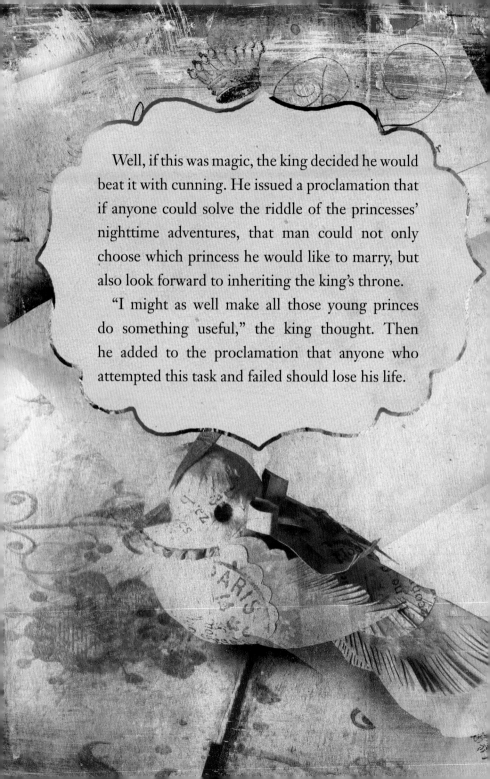

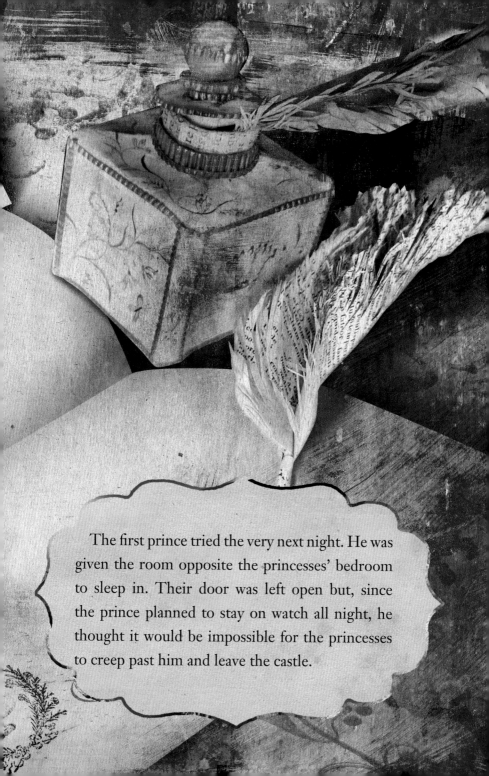

The first prince tried the very next night. He was given the room opposite the princesses' bedroom to sleep in. Their door was left open but, since the prince planned to stay on watch all night, he thought it would be impossible for the princesses to creep past him and leave the castle.

Violette, the eldest princess, brought the prince his supper and a glass of spiced wine. Within minutes, he was fast asleep. Imagine his horror when he woke with a start many hours later! The twelve pairs of ruined slippers reproached him silently for having failed in his task.

The same thing happened the next night and again the next. On the third day, the prince was dispatched.

And so it went on; the palace was soon remarkably empty of young men hoping for a crown and a bride.

CHAPTER THREE

The Soldier

Now it happened that one day a soldier came limping along the road to the palace. He had taken a wound in the wars and been discharged from the army. He had been a brave soldier and fought fiercely for the king, but he was a poor man with not much hope of finding a new job, especially as he was now lame and could not walk far.

He had bread and cheese and apples in his knapsack and rested by the roadside to eat his meager lunch.

An old woman hobbled up and asked if he could spare any food.

"Of course, beldam," he said politely. "You are welcome to half of all I have, but it's not much."

When they had finished their picnic, the old woman said, "Thank you, kind sir. I see you get along not much better than me. Would it not be good to have a warm bed for life, as much food as you could eat and a beautiful young wife?"

"It would be wonderful," said the soldier. "But I'd need a kind fairy to wave her wand to give me that good fortune."

The old woman straightened up, and the soldier thought she looked much younger and stronger than before. She told him the story of the princesses and the riddle of how they disappeared each night to dance their shoes to pieces. She told him of the king, so keen to keep his daughters safe and so puzzled by their strange predicament and their fatigue. "They sleep all day, now, and are no good for anyone or anything," the old woman said. "And the king has offered his kingdom and the hand in marriage of one of the princesses to anyone who can help him solve the mystery."

"I would like to see those twelve lovely princesses," said the soldier.

But when the old woman told him the penalty for failure was death, he shook his head. "I think it would be better if I applied to be a shoemaker in the palace," he said. "It would be safer. I'm done with risking my life."

"You have helped me and shared your food with me," said the old woman. "I can see that you are a brave and good young man and deserve a better future than that of a vagabond. Trust me. Do what I am about to tell you, and do not forget. I promise that you will succeed." She went on, "Just remember to drink nothing the princesses give you. And take this . . ."

The old woman handed the soldier a piece of silky cloth folded as small as a handkerchief.

"When you put it on, you will be invisible," she said. "Then you can follow unseen wherever the princesses go."

The soldier shook out the tiny folded gossamer cloth and saw that the old woman had given him a magic cloak that swirled around his head and shoulders. He could see everything through a shimmery haze — the old woman, who was now looking very beautiful and mysterious, the countryside and, in the distance, the palace where twelve princesses hid their secret.

"I'll do it," he said, taking off the cloak and stowing it carefully inside his jerkin. "Good day to you, ma'am. Wish me luck!"

"You won't need luck," said the strange woman, standing straight and regal as she waved goodbye to him. "The queen's good wishes go with you. Just remember not to drink the wine."

Chapter Four

A Glass of Wine

The king gave the soldier just as warm a welcome as the young princes had received — and some smart new clothes as well.

"He is handsome," whispered little Princess Amandine, peeping out from behind a screen.

"But he can't be a prince," said Princess Violette. "A prince would have come by carriage. And, anyway, he can't walk properly. I saw him limping up the palace steps like a poor, weary traveler."

That night, Princess Violette brought spiced wine to the soldier but she did not see him tip it away in a potted palm. Soon he was yawning and stretching and rubbing his eyes.

"This one is not even going to try," sighed Violette as she and her sisters heard the soldier's snores. "Come, sisters — let's get ready!"

Then all twelve princesses opened the chests that contained their finest clothes and dressed themselves in silk and satins and lace. They wound colored ribbons and shimmering pearls in their hair, picked up fans and flowers, adjusted their coronets of silver and gold, and sprayed one another with expensive perfumes.

Then they finally slid their dainty feet into brand new slippers of green and lavender and blue to match their elaborate dresses.

Princess Violette went to the corner of her bed and tapped the floor with her elegant purple slipper — one, two, three.

"Sleep well, handsome stranger," she called softly. "See you in the morning."

CHAPTER FIVE

An Enchanted Ball

But the soldier was not asleep; he was watching from his room and every nerve in his body was tingling. He was ready to follow the princesses and find out their magic secret. As soon as the eldest princess tapped the floor, he saw her bed swing away and there, where there once had been a bed with satin sheets, was a hidden door that opened to reveal a stone staircase. The soldier flung the magic cloak over his head and followed the disappearing girls. He knew the slightest noise would give him away so, despite his limp and his aching wounded leg, he crept behind the princesses without making a sound.

He was so quick on their heels as the princesses were descending deep below the castle that he trod on the hem of Princess Amandine's lemon taffeta dress.

"Oh!" cried Amandine. "Who is there?" And she sounded so frightened that all the princesses stopped and turned to see what was the matter.

"No one," said her big sister, Princess Violette. She had looked out for Amandine ever since their mother died. "You are imagining it. Come on, we must go quickly." She took Amandine's hand.

The stone staircase led down and down and then out through the cellars of the castle into a wood, where the princesses slipped through the trees like a flock of butterflies.

The soldier followed them. He looked around him, and the trees in the wood glowed silver in the moonlight. At first the soldier thought it was the enchantment of seeing the trees through his shimmering gossamer

cloak of invisibility. But, when he lifted a corner of the cloak, he could see the leaves really were made of silver!

"I'd better take back a twig," thought the soldier "so that the king will believe me."

Crack! The twig of silver leaves snapped off so loudly that the littlest princess turned around, startled. Once more she cried out and once more her eldest sister grabbed her hand and hurried her on, into another wood. The soldier followed silently.

Here the trees had leaves of gold, and the princesses poured through the golden wood like a procession of rainbows. The soldier lifted up the cloak again to see if he was imagining things, but the leaves were as gold as the king's crown. He reached for a low branch and snapped off a twig as quietly as he could, but *crack!* — the sound of the breaking twig was enough to make little Amandine stop in her tracks once again and, once again, Princess Violette had to turn and reassure her littlest sister that all was well.

41

On the princesses glided, and behind them limped
the soldier, as quickly and as noiselessly as he could.
They came to a third wood where all the leaves on
the trees were made of sparkling diamonds. They
tinkled like a million crystal chandeliers as the
princesses swept passed them, brushing them with
their beautiful multicolored dresses. The soldier
felt as if he were in an enchanted dream, watching
the fluttering princesses make their way like a
shower of shooting stars.

He took a twig of diamond leaves that made a
sound like a little chime of bells as he stowed it in
his jerkin with the other twigs. The littlest princess
looked up but, by then, they had all reached the
edge of a lake, and her sisters were all hurrying her
along with them.

Drawn up at the edge of the lake were twelve
slender boats, with a prince sitting in each of them.
Across the other side of the water gleamed a castle
made of white marble, shining with so many lights
that the darkness of the night was banished.

The soldier watched, amazed, as each princess stepped into a boat and was rowed away. The invisible soldier was so astonished at what he saw that he was almost left alone on the lakeside as, one by one, the boats slipped away across the inky lake. But, at the last minute, just as the last boat left the shore, the soldier managed to step into it and crouch down, unseen under his cloak. It was the one Princess Amandine sat in, and she shivered as the boat rocked.

"You are heavier than usual," teased the youngest prince who was rowing the last boat carrying the soldier and Amandine across the water. "What have you been eating?"

When the boats reached the other side of the lake, the princes jumped out and escorted the princesses into a ballroom sparkling with lights and tingling with music. At the far end was a table spread with every delicacy you can imagine: handsome pies, fresh cheeses and fruits, chocolate éclairs, succulent jellies and crisp sorbets. The soldier was hungry by now and very thirsty but dared not eat or drink anything.

He stood and watched the dancing through his magic cloak, feeling very alone as the nimble-footed princes in their fine velvets and brocades whisked and whirled the twelve princesses around the ballroom.

They danced every dance, even the littlest princess with the youngest prince, until the soldier could see that the princesses' slippers were unraveling in strips. Then he knew it was time to go home. And he knew that he would have to get back first. This time, the soldier stepped into the eldest princess's boat so that he could run ahead of them all through the enchanted woods and back up the stone stairs and hurl himself into bed, with the cloak of invisibility stuffed under his pillow.

Across the lake and through the three woods the princesses went, bidding farewell to their night-time dancing partners. The soldier, limping and running ahead of the princesses, the princesses laughing and yawning behind him. They were tired now, but full of chatter and laughter about their night's adventures. Only Amandine thought she heard soft footfalls ahead of them as they made their way home. But she did not want to bother her big sister again.

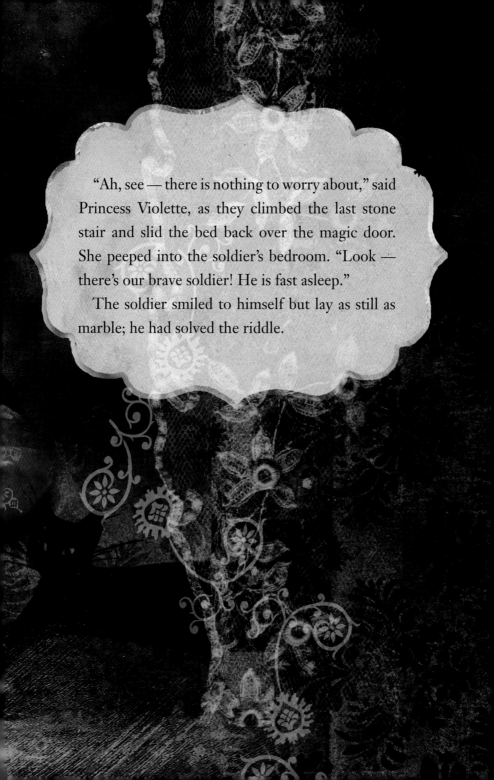

"Ah, see — there is nothing to worry about," said Princess Violette, as they climbed the last stone stair and slid the bed back over the magic door. She peeped into the soldier's bedroom. "Look — there's our brave soldier! He is fast asleep."

The soldier smiled to himself but lay as still as marble; he had solved the riddle.

CHAPTER SIX

The Last Night

For two more nights, the soldier stayed in the room opposite the princesses' bedchamber. Each evening, he pretended to drink the wine that Violette gave him and pretended to be deeply asleep, and each evening, he threw the invisible cloak around him and followed the princesses to their ball. And, for the next two nights, everything happened in exactly the same way, with the mysterious staircase, the journey through the three woods and across the lake, the dancing and feasting in the castle and the shoes worn out before dawn.

But on the third night, as he left the ballroom for the last time, the soldier took a golden wine goblet from the table and hid it in his jerkin.

All that evening, Princess Amandine had been nervous, looking around her as if she could sense the soldier's presence. She no longer dared bother her sisters or ask for Princess Violette's reassurance. She knew that she was hearing sounds she could not explain, and she felt as if there was a ghost at her shoulder all evening, but no one would believe her and she didn't want her older sister to think she was being silly. On this third night, from the corner of her eye, she saw the golden cup suddenly vanish. She was very afraid but she bravely kept her fears to herself.

At the end of the night, as dawn was beginning to creep across the sky, the soldier ran as fast as he could, limping as he always did, up the stone stairs to his bed. His heart was thumping, knowing that this was his last night with the princesses and that in the morning he must convince the king or die.

CHAPTER SEVEN

A Secret Discovered

"My daughters sail to an enchanted castle each night?" said the king the next day. "And dance with princes who are under a spell?"

"Yes, Your Majesty," replied the soldier. "They climb down a staircase under Princess Violette's bed and travel through woods of silver, gold and diamonds."

The soldier laid the three twigs of precious metals and gems in front of the king. "Then they are rowed across the lake and dance all night in the castle," he went on. "I watched them dance for three nights. That's the reason their slippers are in tatters every morning." The soldier took out the golden goblet from his jerkin. He put that on the table too.

He waited for the king to say something. The king looked at what the soldier had laid in front of him. Then he heard a gasp and a rustle of silk in the next door room, and he knew the princesses were listening. The soldier was telling the truth.

The king turned to the soldier. "You have solved my problem at long last," he said. "Which of my daughters will you have?"

"The eldest," said the soldier without hesitation. "It is not right for any of the sisters to marry before Princess Violette, and she will suit me very well. She is always kind to her youngest sister, and I hope she'll be kind to me."

So Princess Violette and the soldier were married. Princess Violette admired the soldier's courage and thought him a good husband. He, in turn, loved her kindness and her laughing eyes, and both Violette and the soldier always had a special place in their hearts for brave little Amandine.

All the eleven sisters were bridesmaids, and Amandine carried her sister's flowers. And, if you looked very closely, you could see, tucked away between the lilies and the roses, the delphiniums and the amaranthus, the marguerites and the veronica, the vervain, the eglantine, the jasmine, the violets and the iris and the almond flowers, there were three sprigs and leaves that were not flowers at all, but were made of gold and silver and diamonds.

That night there was a grand ball in the king's palace, just as glittering as any ever held in the enchanted castle. This time, the soldier needed no magic cloak of invisibility and he danced as if he had never hurt his leg in the war. Even the king danced with each of his daughters in turn till his own shoes were worn out.

CHAPTER SEVEN

All the princes who were left in the kingdom came to the ball, but nothing more was ever heard of the ones under a spell in the castle across the lake. And no one ever found the staircase again; it was sealed up forever once the riddle of the dancing princesses had been solved.